The Shadowed Path Trilogy

Book 1:

Shadows of Innocence

by

Adriano Alamia

Foreword

In a world that often walks the fine line between light and shadow, "Shadows of Innocence" emerges as a beacon, illuminating the depths of human resilience, the complexity of moral choices, and the unyielding strength of familial bonds. Adriano Alamia, with deft storytelling and profound empathy, invites readers on a journey alongside Ethan Harper—a young man thrust into the tumultuous waves of adversity, tasked with the monumental responsibility of protecting his siblings in the wake of unspeakable tragedy.

This narrative is not just a story of survival against the odds; it is a heart-rending exploration of the sacrifices we make for those we love, the burdens we carry in silence, and the indomitable spirit of youth confronted with the darkness of the world. Alamia masterfully crafts a world where every shadow holds a story, every choice carries weight, and every light in the darkness is a testament to the enduring power of hope and love.

"Shadows of Innocence" is a mirror reflecting the struggles many face, often in the quiet corners of life, unseen and unheard. It is a call to recognize the unseen warriors among us—the young shoulders bearing the weight of the world, the silent sufferers finding strength in love, and the resilient hearts battling the unseen and the unspoken.

As you turn these pages, allow yourself to be enveloped in the world of Ethan, Lily, and Max. Their journey is a poignant reminder that even in our darkest moments, we are never truly alone. The path may be shadowed, but it is also scattered with points of light—moments of courage, acts of sacrifice, and the unbreakable bonds that anchor us.

Welcome to a story of shadows, but more importantly, a story of the innocence that shines through them.

Table of Contents

To the unseen warriors,

For those who tread the shadowed paths of life, battling the unseen and the unspoken - this journey is for you – a testament to the resilience of the human spirit and the unbreakable bonds that anchor us in the darkest of times. May these pages echo your courage and whisper hope in the quiet moments of your struggle.

And to my beloved family – my unwavering lighthouse in the stormiest seas. Your love and support always illuminate the path back home.

The Night Everything Changed

The evening had settled over our small town like a soft blanket, tucking in the houses with their glowing windows and the quiet streets. The familiar sound of the living room clock ticking at home was a comforting backdrop to my studies. I sprawled on the couch, a history textbook open in my lap, but the words blurred as my thoughts drifted.

I couldn't shake off the unease that crept over me every time Mom and Dad were out for the evening. They were at a local charity event tonight, and even though they promised to be back by ten, the worry gnawed at me. I've always been the worrier in the family - the one who double-checked the locks at night and made sure the stove was off.

My eleven-year-old sister Lily was at the dining table, her brow furrowed in concentration over a jigsaw puzzle. She had this way of biting her lip when focused, a habit she'd had since she was little. And then there was Max, my nine-year-old brother, the family's bundle of energy. He was in the living room; constructing a fort from every pillow and blanket he could find.

"Max, don't make too much of a mess," I called out, my voice carrying that mix of annoyance and affection that only older brothers know.

He just laughed; his voice muffled from within his fortress of cushions. "I'm building a castle, Ethan!"

I smiled, shaking my head: Max and his castles. I remember building forts with Dad when I was his age, pretending we were knights defending our kingdom. The memory brought a bittersweet ache. I glanced at the clock: 8:45 PM. It was still over an hour until Mom and Dad would be home.

I focused on my textbook, a detailed account of the Civil War. However, the words seemed to dance and weave, forming images of cannon smoke and charging soldiers that morphed into the worried faces of my parents. I closed the book, rubbing my eyes. It was no use; I couldn't concentrate.

The sounds of the house were a symphony I knew by heart—the ticking clock, the soft scraping of puzzle pieces, Max's muffled giggle from his fort. But then, a new sound, out of place and time—a gentle creak of the front door opening.

My head snapped up, heart racing. It was too early for Mom and Dad. A shadow stretched across the hall floor, a dark, unfamiliar silhouette against the dim street lights outside. Fear tightened its grip around my chest.

I stood up, letting the textbook fall to the floor with a thud. Lily looked up, her eyes wide, and Max poked his head out from his fortress of cushions, his face a mix of curiosity and concern.

"Who is it?" Lily's voice quivered slightly, barely above a whisper.

I edged towards the door; every sense heightened. Through the peephole, I saw a police officer. My heart sank to my stomach. Police officers don't show up at your door late at night with good news.

I opened the door slowly, bracing myself. The officer's face was kind but carried a weight of sorrow that made my knees weak.

"Good evening, son. Are you Ethan Harper?" His voice was soft, but it filled the room, heavy with unspoken dread.

"Yes, sir. That's me. What's going on?" My voice was steady, but a storm was brewing inside—a whirlwind of fear and anticipation.

The officer's eyes held mine, and I saw a deep sadness telling me that whatever he said would change everything.

"There's been an accident, son. Your parents..." He paused, the words catching in his throat as if they were too painful to release.

A cold wave of terror washed over me. "No," I whispered, a futile denial. "They were just..."

The officer stepped closer, his hand reaching to rest on my shoulder. "I'm sorry, Ethan. Your parents' car - there was an accident. They didn't make it."

Those words shattered the world as I knew it. I stumbled backward, my back hitting the wall. My mind screamed in denial, but the truth was there in his eyes and words.

Lily's cry broke through my shock. She had risen from her seat, her puzzle forgotten, her face pale with fear. Max emerged from his fort, his eyes wide and uncomprehending.

As I slid down the wall, what happened began to sink in. Parents don't just go out and not come back. That occurs in other families, in movies, but not in us. But the officer's solemn face, the undeniable truth in his words, said otherwise.

"Ethan?" Lily's voice was small, terrified. "What did he say? Where are Mom and Dad?"

I looked up, my eyes meeting those of my siblings. In their faces, I saw my fear reflected on me. And in that moment, I understood that everything had changed. I was no longer just their brother. I was all they had left.

A New Dawn

The sun rose the following day with cruel indifference, its rays spilling into the living room where we had fallen asleep, a tangle of limbs and tear-streaked faces. I woke with a start, the events of the night flooding back in a relentless wave. Mom and Dad are gone. The reality hit me anew, and I couldn't breathe momentarily.

Lily curled up against my side, her eyes red-rimmed and puffy from crying. Max was asleep, his tiny chest rising and falling evenly, one arm flung over my waist. In sleep, he looked peaceful, untouched by the tragedy that had upended our lives.

I gently disentangled myself from their grasp, my body stiff and aching. The police officer,

Officer Daniels, had stayed with us through the night, sitting in his patrol car outside. He had offered to call anyone who could come, but there was no one. Our relatives were few and far between, scattered across the country, distant in miles and relationships.

The house felt different that morning, as if it, too, mourned the loss of its heart and soul. I made my way to the kitchen, my steps echoing in the silence. The everyday task of making breakfast, which Mom used to do with a song on her lips, now fell on me.

As I scrambled eggs and toasted bread, my mind raced. What were we going to do? I was just fifteen, barely more than a kid myself. How was I supposed to take care of Lily and Max? The threat of foster care loomed over us like a dark cloud. I wouldn't let that happen.

I set the plates on the table, the clinking of cutlery a harsh sound in the quiet morning. I called out softly, waking Lily and Max. They stumbled into the kitchen, their eyes still heavy with sleep and sorrow.

We ate silently, the usual morning chatter replaced by a thick, unspoken grief. I tried to put on a brave face for Lily and Max, but every bite was an effort, each swallow a reminder of the emptiness at our table.

After breakfast, I cleared the dishes mechanically, my thoughts a jumbled mess. I needed to figure out what to do next. The school and the authorities would all need to be informed. But more than that, I required a plan, a way to keep us together, to keep us safe.

The doorbell rang, slicing through the silence. I tensed, a surge of anxiety rising in my chest. Was it someone from social services? A neighbor? Reluctantly, I made my way to the door.

Standing on the doorstep was Mrs. Henderson, our next-door neighbor. She was a kind woman in her sixties, always quick with a smile or a helping hand. Today, her eyes filled with tears, her usual cheer replaced by solemn sympathy.

"Oh, Ethan," she said, her voice breaking as she hugged me. "I just heard. I'm so, so sorry."

We stood there momentarily; her embrace a small comfort in a world that had turned cold and unforgiving. She pulled back, her hands gripping mine.

"If there's anything I can do, just let me know, okay?" she said, her earnestness clear in her watery eyes.

I nodded, unable to find the words to thank her. She promised to come by later with some groceries and left, her grief for our loss evident in her slow, heavy steps.

The rest of the morning passed in a blur: phone calls to the school, awkward conversations explaining our situation, and assurances that we were okay and managed. But with each call, the reality of our situation became more apparent. We were on our own, and the road ahead was daunting.

In the afternoon, Officer Daniels returned. He had taken care of the formalities, the reports, and the necessary notifications. He also brought news that a social worker would soon be visiting us. The mention of foster care made my stomach churn. I couldn't let that happen. I had to find a way to keep us together.

As I tucked Lily and Max into bed that evening, I felt the weight of responsibility settling on my shoulders. I promised them I would do everything possible to keep us together and protect them. They nodded, their eyes filled with a trust that warmed and terrified me.

After they fell asleep, I sat at the kitchen table, a notepad in front of me. I began to make a list, a plan. We needed money to prove that I could take care of us. I thought about getting a job, but what job would be enough? Then, a dangerous and frightening idea came to me, but it promised us the necessary solution.

A Dangerous Proposition

The next day dawned with deceptive normalcy, the sun casting its golden glow over a world that felt irrevocably altered. I had spent most of the night awake, my mind racing with plans and fears. The idea that had taken root was risky, but I couldn't see another way out. I had to protect Lily and Max, no matter what.

After making breakfast and getting the kids ready, I sent them to school. Their hesitant steps and backward glances tore at my heart. I promised them I'd be there when they got back, a promise I intended to keep, no matter the cost.

Once they were gone, I took a deep breath and headed out. There was a place I needed to go, a person I needed to see. Someone who, rumor had it, could offer the kind of help I was desperately seeking.

The streets were busier now, filled with the hustle of daily life. People were going about their routines, oblivious to the turmoil inside me. I walked with purpose; my destination cleared in my mind: the outskirts of town, where tidy homes and manicured lawns gave way to grittier, more industrial landscapes.

I found myself outside an unassuming building, the kind that you'd pass without a second glance. I hesitated, my hand hovering over the door. This was it, the point of no return. Taking a deep breath, I pushed the door open and stepped inside.

The interior was dimly lit, and the air was heavy with the scent of oil and metal. A figure emerged from the shadows, commanding even in the gloom.

You're Ethan, right?" His voice was deep, gravelly. He knew who I was, which meant he had been expecting me.

"Yes," I replied, my voice steady despite my heart pounding. "I heard you can help people... in my situation."

He eyed me, a flicker of interest passing over his features. "Maybe I can, maybe I can't. It depends on what you're willing to do."

I swallowed hard, the weight of my decision pressing down on me. "I'll do whatever it takes to keep my family together."

He nodded slowly as if he had heard this kind of resolve before. "All right, kid. Let's talk business."

We sat at a battered table, the room around us fading into the background. He laid out the terms, speaking in a matter-of-fact tone that belied the gravity of a proposal.

It was simple yet chilling – work for him as an enforcer, a collector of debts. The pay was more than I could have hoped for, enough to keep Lily and Max comfortable and out of the clutches of foster care. But the work was dangerous, illegal, and would stain my soul.

I listened, each word a heavy stone in my stomach. I thought of Lily and Max, their faces the last thing I saw before entering this shadowy world.

When he finished explaining, he leaned back, watching me with an unreadable expression. "Well, kid? You in or out?"

I thought of my parents and the life they wanted for us. Would they understand? Would they forgive me for the choices I was about to make? I pushed these thoughts aside. This was about survival, about keeping the only family I had left.

"I'm in," I said, my voice a whisper of resolve.

He nodded, a hint of a smile playing on his lips. "Good. You start tonight. Be here at eight. And Ethan," he added, his tone turning serious, "once you're in, there's no turning back. Make sure you're ready for that."

As I left the building, the bright light of day seemed harsh and unforgiving. The weight of my decision settled heavily on my shoulders. I had just agreed to enter a world of darkness, of moral ambiguity, all to keep my siblings safe and together. The irony wasn't lost on me – to preserve our innocence; I was stepping into a role that was anything but innocent.

Walking back home, I felt like a different person. The carefree life I once knew, filled with school projects and simple family joys, was handled like a distant dream. Now, I was to lead a double life – by day, a high school student, striving to maintain the facade of normalcy; by night, an enforcer in a dangerous world.

As I neared home, I saw Lily and Max playing in the yard, their laughter contrasting with the storm raging inside me. I forced a smile, hiding the turmoil and fear that gripped me. They ran towards me, their faces bright with the joy of seeing their brother. At that moment, I knew I had made the right decision. For them, I would walk through the fire and wade through the darkness. I would do anything.

Double Life

The internal chasm within me widened with each day, my existence a precarious balance between light and shadow. By day, I was Ethan Harper, the quintessential high school honors student whose life was a canvas of normalcy and adolescent routines. Yet, beneath this veneer of ordinary teenage life, a storm of complexity and moral ambiguity churned incessantly.

Nightly, as I stepped into the murky world that Mr. Kline had introduced me to, I felt the erosion of my soul. Each task I undertook—each debt collected; each message delivered—was a departure from the person I aspired to be. The justification that it was all for Lily and Max, to provide them with stability and keep the specter of foster care at bay, was a mantra I repeated to silence the burgeoning guilt. But the truth was, with every action that plunged me deeper into this clandestine existence, a piece of my innocence was stripped away, leaving me to question who I truly was beneath the facade.

The duality of my life became a consuming force. At school, where I once thrived effortlessly, focusing became a herculean task. The mundanities of high school life—classes, friendships, extracurriculars—felt increasingly alien, as if I were viewing my own life from the other side of a glass, darkly. I wore the mask of normalcy, a facade crafted for the sake of Lily and Max, ensuring their world remained untouched by the shadows that had claimed mine.

Their innocence was a stark contrast to the world I navigated by night. They lived in a realm of simplicity and joy, untouched by the complexities and moral quandaries that haunted me. The burden of my secret life, the weight of the choices I made, rested solely on my shoulders—a secret pact with darkness to ensure their light remained unblemished.

As I became more entrenched in Mr. Kline's world, taking on tasks that blurred the lines between right and wrong further, the toll on my conscience grew. Each night, returning home felt like crossing from one universe to another, a journey back to a semblance of normalcy that was increasingly hard to reconcile with the person I was becoming.

The night Lily confronted me, her eyes brimming with concern and confusion, marked a turning point. The simplicity of her question, "Ethan, where do you go every night?" was a mirror reflecting the complexity of my double life. My evasion, a vague mention of a part-time job, was a flimsy veil over a truth too dark to disclose. The weight of that lie, the burden of deceiving those I loved most, was a heavy shackle around my heart.

Despite the facade of academic success and leadership as class president—a role that demanded much of me and further complicated my life—the internal conflict was unrelenting. The dichotomy of my existence was a constant battle, a struggle between the person I was by day and the one I became by night.

Sitting in my room one quiet evening, the reality of my situation settled around me with a clarity that was both liberating and terrifying. The acknowledgment that I could not sustain this double life indefinitely was a truth I had long avoided. The realization that a choice loomed on the horizon—a choice between the darkness and the light, between the path I had stumbled upon and the future I yearned for—was an inevitability I could no longer ignore.

The depth of my internal turmoil, the guilt over the lives I impacted, and the fear of the inevitable decision I must make, were a tempest that threatened to consume me. Yet, in the heart of that storm, a resolve began to crystallize—a determination to find a way back to the light, for Lily, for Max, and for the remnants of the person I once hoped to be.

Unraveling Secrets

Time continued its relentless march, and the strain of my double life grew with each passing day. The mask I wore at school became more challenging to maintain, the weight of my nightly activities a constant shadow looming over me. I lived in a perpetual state of vigilance, always looking over my shoulder and anticipating Mr. Kline's next call.

Lily and Max, blissfully unaware of the life I led outside our home, continued to thrive. They were doing well in school, and their laughter filled the house, starkly contrasting the silence that enveloped me in my solitary moments.

One afternoon, as I was leaving school, I noticed a car parked across the street that I had seen a few too many times in the past week. A chill ran down my spine. Was I being followed? The possibility had always been lurking, but now it seemed a reality. I quickened my pace, my mind racing with potential scenarios.

At home, I tried to act normal, but the fear of being watched my secret life gnawed at me. I kept a vigilant eye on Lily and Max; the thought of them being in danger because of me was unbearable.

That night, as I lay in bed, unable to sleep, I heard a noise downstairs. My heart leaped to my throat. I grabbed the baseball bat under my bed and crept down the stairs. The house was dark; the only sound was the quiet hum of the refrigerator.

As I reached the living room, I saw a shadow move. Adrenaline surged as I raised the bat, ready to defend my home and family. But then a voice stopped me in my tracks.

"Ethan? What are you doing?"

It was Lily, her eyes wide with fear and confusion. She had gotten up to get a glass of water and was surprised to find me looming in the darkness, a bat raised in my hands.

The situation was absurd, almost comical, but the fear in Lily's eyes was real. I lowered the bat, my heart still pounding. I explained that I had heard a noise and was checking. She seemed to accept the explanation, but the look in her eyes told me she knew there was more.

The incident left me shaken. My world, the dangerous path I had chosen, was creeping too close to the one thing I was trying to protect — my family. I realized then that I couldn't keep living like this, constantly in fear, always putting them at risk.

The next day at school, I couldn't focus. My mind was a whirlwind of thoughts, of plans to escape this life I had trapped myself in. But how? I was too deep with Mr. Kline, and I knew that walking away wouldn't be accessible if possible.

The school counselor, Mrs. Jenkins, interrupted my thoughts by calling me into her office. She had noticed a change in my behavior and distractedness and was concerned. I brushed off her concerns with practiced ease, but inside, I screamed for help.

As I walked home that day, I knew a decision must be made. I couldn't keep risking my family's safety; I couldn't keep living a lie. But the fear of what leaving my night job would mean for us — the loss of income, the potential exposure, the danger — was overwhelming.

The Crossroads

Days I melted into nights, each passing hour a testament to my fraying nerves. My life, once simple and filled with the typical concerns of a teenager, had become a labyrinth of lies and danger. The constant fear of my secret life being exposed was like a relentless and suffocating shadow that clung to me.

Lily and Max, the two people for whom I had ventured down this perilous path, were not oblivious to the change in me. I saw it in Lily's hesitant glances, her eyes clouded with worry, in the way Max's once boisterous laughter had softened into a reserved quiet. The burden of my double life was casting a dark veil over their innocence, and the guilt gnawed at me incessantly.

One evening, as I was gearing up for another night under Mr. Kline's command, Lily stopped me at the door. Her voice was filled with fear and courage: "Ethan, what's happening to you? You're always so tense, and every night, you're gone. It's like you're here, but not really. I'm worried about you."

Her words struck deep, a stark reminder of the reality that I was trying to shield her from how I longed to confide in her, to share the crushing weight of my secret. But the truth was a Pandora's box that, once opened, could endanger us all. So, I lied, cloaking my response in half-truths. "It's just school and a part-time job, Lil. I'm fine."

The job that night was meant to be straightforward – a simple collection of dues. But the reality was far from it. The target, a man with a desperate look in his eyes, lashed out violently. The confrontation spiraled out of control, and I found myself in a physical struggle. Adrenaline and survival instincts kicked in, but not without consequences.

I managed to escape, but not unscathed. Bruises painted my skin, and a cut above my eye reminded me of the night's ordeal. The pain was secondary to the shock and realization of the monster I was becoming in the name of protection.

Slipping into the house, I avoided any noise that might wake Lily and Max. The bathroom mirror reflected a stranger at me – a young man marred by the night's violence, a stark contrast to the brother I endeavored to be. Cleaning my wounds in silence, I grappled with the reality of my existence. This wasn't who I wanted to be.

The next day at school, I walked the halls like a specter, my body present but my spirit lost in a tumultuous sea of thoughts. The previous night's events echoed in my mind, a constant, unrelenting reminder that I had to find a way out. Yet, the fear of Mr. Kline's retribution held me in a vice-like grip.

My internal struggle was interrupted by an unexpected encounter. Officer Daniels, the same officer who had been there on the night that altered our lives forever, requested to see me. His visit to the school was out of the ordinary, and his expression was one of concern mixed with professional obligation.

He laid his cards on the table in a quiet office, away from prying eyes and ears. "Ethan, there are rumors about you being involved in unsavory activities. I've seen kids go down this path before. I don't want to see you become another statistic. I'm here to help, not to handcuff."

His words were a lifeline thrown into the turbulent waters of my life. Denial was my immediate refuge, a knee-jerk reaction to protect my secret. But his warning was clear

– my double life was not as hidden as I had hoped.

Returning home that day, the weight of my world was physically on my shoulders. The realization that I couldn't continue this way was as clear as the setting sun. I had to make a choice, and the time was now.

That night, in the solitude of my room, I made a decision. I had to confront Mr. Kline to negotiate somehow my way out of the darkness I had stepped into. It was a risk, a gamble with potentially dire consequences. But the alternative – continuing down this path – was a fate I could no longer accept.

Confronting Shadows

The decision to confront Mr. Kline had been made in the dead of night, a resolution forged in desperation and fear. As the new day dawned, the gravity of that decision weighed heavily on me. The morning routine with Lily and Max felt like a pantomime; each act performed with mechanical precision, my mind a tumultuous sea of what-ifs and maybes.

After sending them off to school, I found myself alone, the house's silence echoing my internal turmoil. The clock ticked mockingly, each second a reminder of the impending confrontation. I had to plan to anticipate every possible outcome of my meeting with Mr. Kline.

Walking through the empty streets to our agreed meeting place, I rehearsed the conversation. My plea to Mr. Kline to let me go, to release me from the obligations that were suffocating me, felt like a fragile hope clutched in a clenched fist.

The meeting place was the same unassuming building where my journey into the underworld had begun. Stepping inside, the familiar scent of oil and metal filled my nostrils, a sensory reminder of the path I had walked.

Mr. Kline was waiting for me, his imposing figure silhouetted against the dim lighting. His eyes, always sharp and calculating, seemed to bore into me as if he could read the tumult in my soul.

"Ethan," he began, his voice a steady rumble, "I hope you have good news for me."

I swallowed hard, steadying my nerves. "Mr. Kline, I need to leave. I can't do this anymore. It's not the life I want or my siblings deserve."

A thick and palpable silence fell over the room. Mr. Kline leaned back, his expression unreadable. "You knew what this was when you signed up. You've been well compensated. People don't just walk away from this life, Ethan."

His words were a cold splash of reality. I knew the risks and the potential for retaliation, but I had to stand my ground. "I understand the risks but must put my family first. I'll pay back whatever I owe. I want out."

Mr. Kline's gaze hardened. "It's not about the money, Ethan. It's about loyalty, about trust. You leave, you break that trust. There are consequences to such actions."

The threat in his words was clear, and a shiver ran down my spine. I had anticipated this, yet the fear it invoked was real and palpable. "I understand, but I'm willing to face those consequences. My family's safety comes first."

For a long moment, Mr. Kline remained silent, his eyes locked on mine. Then, slowly, he nodded. "All right, Ethan. I'll let you go. But remember, if you cross me or speak a word of this to anyone, the consequences won't just fall on you."

I nodded, a mix of relief and lingering fear coursing through me. The meeting ended, and I stepped out into the daylight, feeling like a man reprieved yet acutely aware that the shadows of my past might never fully recede.

A Fragile Peace

The walk back from my meeting with Mr. Kline was a journey through conflicting emotions. Relief, fear, and uncertainty battled within me, each vying for dominance. The threat of Mr. Kline's words lingered in the air, an invisible shroud that threatened to suffocate my newfound sense of freedom.

As I approached our home, the sight of it brought a surge of protectiveness. With its peeling paint and creaky porch, this house was our sanctuary, the only piece of stability Lily, Max, and I had in a world turned upside down. I vowed to do everything in my power to keep it, and them, safe.

Once inside, the quiet starkly contrasted the turmoil in my heart. I moved through the house, each room echoing with memories of laughter and tears. I prepared an early dinner in the kitchen, finding a semblance of normalcy in the routine. The act of cooking, something so mundane, was grounding, a tether to the life I desperately tried to reclaim.

When Lily and Max returned from school, their chatter and laughter filled the house, dispelling some of the shadows that clung to my soul. I watched them, their innocence a stark reminder of the world I had just left behind.

Dinner was a simple affair, but sitting together and sharing a meal felt like a healing ritual. We discussed their day at school, the mundane details a balm to my frayed nerves. I avoided their curious glances, knowing questions about my bruises and the changes in my behavior would come. But for now, I was content to bask in the normalcy of the moment.

After dinner, while Lily and Max did their homework, I retreated to my room, the day's weight pressing down on me. I sat at my desk, the textbooks in front of me a reminder of the life I was fighting to preserve. School, once a place of ambition and dreams, now felt like a battlefield where I resisted for a future for my siblings and me.

That night, sleep eluded me. The darkness of my room was a canvas for my thoughts, painting scenes of what might come. The danger from my association with Mr. Kline wasn't erased; it was merely lurking in the shadows, waiting. I knew that my decision to leave that world behind was just the beginning of a new set of challenges.

I thought about Officer Daniels' warning, the concern in his eyes. Others had noticed my changes and might pose questions I needed more time to answer. The thought of involving Lily and Max in any of this was unbearable. I had to keep them safe, even if it meant keeping them in the dark.

The next few days were a delicate dance of maintaining appearances and watching for any signs of retribution from Mr. Kline's world. I attended school, participated in class, and even tried to rekindle old friendships that had frayed in the past months. But beneath the surface, I was on high alert, my senses attuned to any hint of danger.

In the evenings, I spent time with Lily and Max, playing games, helping with homework, and trying to make up for the weeks of neglect. Their smiles were my sanctuary, their laughter a reminder of what I was fighting for.

While walking home from school one afternoon, I felt the prickle of being watched. I glanced over my shoulder, catching a glimpse of a figure disappearing around a corner. Paranoia, a constant companion, gnawed at my insides. Was it someone from Mr. Kline's world keeping tabs on me? Or was it just a trick of my anxious mind?

The sense of being followed dissipated as I reached home, but the unease remained. I locked the door behind me, a symbolic gesture more than an absolute safeguard. The fragile peace I had found was delicate, and I knew it could shatter at any moment.

Shadows Linger

The days that followed were steeped in a deceptive calm. The routine of school and home life, once mundane, now felt like a tightrope walk above a chasm of potential chaos. The fear of Mr. Kline's retribution was a constant companion, a shadow that followed me through the halls of school and the streets of our neighborhood.

I found myself scrutinizing every face, every car that lingered too long on our street. Paranoia had become my unwelcome ally, whispering warnings and fanning the flames of my anxiety. The glimpse of someone following me the other day had unsettled me more than I cared to admit.

At school, I tried to keep up appearances. I participated in class discussions, laughed at jokes, and even managed to run a student council meeting. But it all felt like an act, a performance put on for the benefit of an unseen audience. My classmates were oblivious to the turmoil beneath my calm exterior, unaware of the danger lurking outside our doors.

Returning home each day, I found solace in Lily and Max's presence. Their innocence starkly contrasted with the world I had entangled myself in. I made a concerted effort to be more present for them to compensate for the time lost to my nocturnal activities. We played board games and watched movies, and I helped them with their homework, cherishing these moments of normalcy.

One evening, as I was tucking them into bed, Max looked up at me with his big, trusting eyes. "Ethan, are you okay? You seem sad sometimes."

His question caught me off guard, a piercing arrow to the facade I had carefully constructed. I mustered a smile and ruffled his hair. "I'm okay, buddy. I'm just tired from school and stuff. Don't worry about me."

But Max's question lingered long after I left their room. The burden of my secrets was not just mine to bear; it was seeping into their lives, casting a pall over our home.

The nights were the hardest. Alone in my room, the silence was oppressive, filled with the echoes of my thoughts. I lay awake, staring at the ceiling, playing over scenarios of what might happen if Mr. Kline decided I was a loose end that needed tying up. The fear for my safety was secondary to the terror of what could happen to Lily and Max.

I thought about reaching out to Officer Daniels, but the risk of exposing my siblings to the criminal world I had been a part of held me back. I felt trapped in a web of my own making, each strand a decision that had led me here.

The semblance of normalcy at school and home was shattered one afternoon when I received a text message that chilled me to the bone. It was from an unknown number, but the message was clear: "We're watching."

Panic coursed through me as I scanned the school courtyard, looking for any sign of who might have sent it. Was it a warning from Mr. Kline? A threat? Or someone else who had discovered my secret? The ambiguity of the message was its form of torture.

I lay in bed that night, the message replaying in my mind. The sense of being watched and followed was now a palpable presence. I realized that stepping away from Mr. Kline's world was more complex than I had hoped. The shadows of my past lingered, threatening to engulf the fragile peace I had tried to build.

Unseen Eyes

The threatening text message unleashed a storm of paranoia and fear that I couldn't quell. At school, my eyes constantly darted to the windows, doors, and sea of faces in the hallways. Each shadow, each unknown number that called my phone, set my heart racing. The sanctuary of normalcy I had tried to build was crumbling around me, and I felt exposed and vulnerable.

In class, my mind was a whirlwind of anxiety. I couldn't focus on the teacher's words; they were distant echoes against the thundering beat of my own heart. The once familiar faces of my classmates now seemed alien, potential harbingers of danger.

Walking home became a tactical exercise, each step measured, each route planned to avoid long stretches of solitude. The crisp autumn air, once a refreshing respite, now felt cold and biting, as if it, too, had turned against me.

At home, I became overly vigilant, double-checking locks and windows, much to the curiosity of Lily and Max. "Why are you checking the locks so much, Ethan?" Lily asked one evening, her brow furrowed in concern.

I brushed off her question with a forced laugh. "Just being careful. You know, it's always good to be safe." But my nonchalant tone was a thin veil over my mounting dread.

The warning, "We're watching," echoed in my mind constantly. It was a leash, a reminder of the invisible eyes that might be monitoring my every move. The sense of being watched was an oppressive shroud, stifling the freedom I longed for.

Sleep became a luxury I couldn't afford. My nights were restless, filled with the sounds of the house settling, each creak and groan a potential harbinger of danger. The darkness of my room was no longer a haven but a canvas for my fears, painting scenarios of harm befalling Lily and Max.

One day, as I walked through the park on my way home, the sense of being followed reached a crescendo. I could almost feel the eyes on me, a tangible weight on my back. Turning quickly, I saw a figure darting behind a tree. My heart pounded in my chest as I considered confronting the stalker. However, the risk of a possibly violent confrontation held me back.

Instead, I quickened my pace, my mind racing with questions. Was this Mr. Kline's doing? Or had my activities attracted the attention of someone else in his world? The uncertainty was maddening.

As I sat in the living room pretending to watch TV with Lily and Max that evening, my thoughts were elsewhere. My siblings' laughter and light-hearted chatter were a distant melody, overshadowed by the dissonant chords of my anxiety.

I needed to take action to confront this threat head-on. But the fear of dragging Lily and Max into the danger outside our door paralyzed me. I felt trapped in a maze with no apparent exit, every path leading to potential peril.

The house's silence starkly contrasted with the chaos in my mind. The message's implications were clear – I was not free from Mr. Kline's grip. The life I had tried to leave behind was still entwined with my present, a serpent coiled around the foundation of our home.

Breaking Point

With each passing day, the walls of our home felt like they were closing in, a physical manifestation of the pressure that was building inside me. The weight of the unseen threat hanging over us was like a heavy cloak, stifling and inescapable. I found myself jumping at the slightest sounds, a door creaking, a floorboard groaning, each noise a potential harbinger of the danger I feared would come crashing into our lives.

Amid this turmoil, Lily and Max continued their daily routines, unaware of the storm brewing. I watched them, a mix of admiration for their resilience and guilt for the secrets I was keeping. Their laughter, once a source of comfort, now sounded like a distant echo, muffled by the cacophony of my fears.

At school, my focus was scattered, my thoughts a tangled web of anxiety and plans. I sat in classes, my eyes fixed on the pages of textbooks, but the words were just ink on paper, meaningless in the face of my growing dread. Conversations with friends became a labyrinth of evasion as I tried to avoid any questions that might lead to the truth.

One afternoon, as I walked the familiar path home, the sensation of being watched was overwhelming. Every shadow seemed to move, and every whisper of wind sounded like footsteps behind me. I quickened my pace, my heart pounding in my chest. The need to see Lily and Max to ensure their safety drove me forward.

As I reached our front door, I paused, my hand on the doorknob, bracing myself for what might be waiting inside. The house was quiet, too quiet. Stepping in, I called for Lily and Max, my voice echoing through the empty hallway. There was no response, just the silence that answered back.

Panic surged through me as I rushed from room to room, the fear that had been simmering beneath the surface now boiling over. It was only when I found a note from Lily on the kitchen table, saying they had gone to a friend's house, that I could breathe again.

That night, as I lay in bed, the events of the past weeks played over in my mind like a nightmarish film. The threatening message, the constant feeling of being watched, and the fear for my siblings' safety were all converging to a breaking point. I couldn't live like this, constantly looking over my shoulder, waiting for the other shoe to drop.

I realized then that I had to take control of the situation. I couldn't let this unseen threat dictate our lives, nor let the fear of what might happen paralyze me any longer. It was time to confront this head-on, to root out the danger and eliminate it.

The following day, I set out with a newfound resolve. My first stop was at the school, where I asked to meet with Officer Daniels. The walk to his office was like walking through a fog, each step bringing me closer to a confrontation I had long avoided.

Sitting across from Officer Daniels, I felt a sense of relief mixed with apprehension. I didn't divulge everything, but I shared enough to convey our sense of danger. His expression turned grave as he listened, his eyes reflecting concern and a determination to help.

"We need to take this seriously, Ethan. If you're being threatened, it's not something you should face alone," Officer Daniels said, his voice firm. He promised to look into the matter, to provide discreet surveillance around our home, and to keep an eye out for any suspicious activity.

Leaving his office, I felt a weight lift off my shoulders, albeit slightly. There was still much to do and many uncertainties to navigate, but I felt like I wasn't alone in this fight for the first time in weeks.

Confronting the Past

The decision to involve Officer Daniels had set in motion a chain of events that felt terrifying and liberating. I felt apprehension and resolve as I walked home from school that day. Once a gauntlet of shadows and fears, the streets now seemed a little less daunting, knowing that eyes were watching over us for our protection.

Lily and Max were their usual selves at home, blissfully unaware of the protective gaze that now encompassed our house. I watched them play in the backyard, a sense of urgency propelling my next steps. It was time to face my past, to confront the source of our danger.

After ensuring Lily and Max were safely tucked into bed that evening, I set out. My destination was a place I had hoped never to return to, the heart of the world I had tried to leave behind. The streets grew darker and more desolate as I ventured into the rougher part of town, where Mr. Kline's operations had their roots.

The building loomed ahead, a monolith in the dim light. My heart pounded in my chest; each beat a reminder of what was at stake. I had to know if Mr. Kline was behind the threats or if my actions had attracted someone else's attention in his world.

Stepping inside, the familiar scent of oil and metal assaulted my senses, a stark reminder of the nights spent under its oppressive roof. The hallways were deserted, the usual buzz of activity eerily absent. My footsteps echoed off the walls, a solitary sound in the void.

I found Mr. Kline in his office, dimly lit with shadows clinging to the corners. He looked up, surprise etched on his features at my unannounced appearance.

"Ethan, this is a surprise," he said, his voice a blend of curiosity and caution. "To what do I owe this unexpected visit?"

I took a deep breath, steadying my nerves. "I need to know if you're behind the threats, the messages. My family is in danger because of my past with you. I need to know if that danger is coming from you."

Mr. Kline leaned back in his chair, studying me. "Ethan, you left this world. I gave you my word I wouldn't come after you. I keep my word." His tone was matter-of-fact, but there was a flicker of something else in his eyes — perhaps respect.

"Then someone else knows about me, about what I did," I said, the realization settling like lead in my stomach.

Mr. Kline nodded slowly. "It's possible. You made an impression in the short time you were here. Some might not take kindly to your sudden departure."

I felt a chill run down my spine. The network of criminals and shadowy figures I had briefly participated in was extensive and complex. Anyone could be a potential threat.

"Be careful, Ethan. You stepped out of this world, but shadows from it can still reach out," Mr. Kline warned, his voice low.

The conversation with Mr. Kline had confirmed my fears. I was not just fighting against one known enemy but against an unseen, unknown threat that had emerged from the shadows of my past.

As I walked home, my mind raced with plans and contingencies. I had to be vigilant and protect Lily and Max from the invisible dangers lurking in the darkness. My past choices weighed heavily on me, but my resolve to keep my siblings safe was firm.

Gathering Storm

As the days slipped by, the sense of impending danger grew. My conversations with Mr. Kline had offered no concrete solutions, only the confirmation of my worst fears. The world I had once been a part of was vast and shadowy, and now it felt like its many eyes were fixed upon us.

I constantly looked over my shoulder, analyzing every face in the crowd for signs of recognition or threat. My nights were filled with strategy and planning, mapping out routes to and from school, identifying safe places in the neighborhood, and rehearsing emergency plans with Lily and Max under the guise of a game.

At school, my facade of normalcy was cracking. Friends began noticing my distant demeanor and frequent, anxious glances at my phone. "Ethan, is everything okay? You seem a little off," my friend Jenna asked one day, her brow creased in concern.

I forced a smile, spinning a tale of stress from schoolwork and the responsibilities of being class president. Jenna seemed to accept this, but her worried gaze lingered a moment too long.

Each day, as I walked home, the ordinary sights and sounds of the neighborhood took on a sinister tone. The rustling leaves sounded like whispers, and the sun's shadows seemed to hide threats. I hurried my steps, eager to return to the safety of our home, to see Lily and Max's faces and assure myself they were still safe.

One evening, as I prepared dinner, the phone rang. My heart skipped a beat as I saw an unknown number on the display. Steeling myself, I answered, my voice steady but my hand trembling.

The voice on the other end was distorted, almost mechanical. "You can't hide, Ethan. We know where you are. We know where your siblings are." The call ended abruptly, leaving a chilling silence in its wake.

Panic surged through me, a torrential wave threatening to sweep away my composure. I looked out the window, half expecting to see a figure lurking in the shadows. But there was nothing, just the quiet street and the fading light of the day.

That night, I sat in my room, the phone call replaying. The threat was no longer abstract; it was real and immediate. I had to act to find a way to end this once and for all. The safety of Lily and Max was my only priority.

I reached out to Officer Daniels, my voice steady as I recounted the phone call. He listened intently, his responses measured and calm. "We'll increase surveillance around your house, Ethan. And I'll see what more we can do. Stay alert, and keep your phone close."

The darkness around me felt oppressive, a physical manifestation of the fear and uncertainty that engulfed us. I knew the next few days, perhaps even hours, would be crucial. The storm that had been gathering was about to break, and I had to be ready to face whatever it brought.

The Siege

The dawn broke with an ominous feeling that day, a prelude to the turmoil about unfolding. As I prepared breakfast, my mind was a battlefield of strategies and what-ifs. The phone call from the previous night had shattered any illusions of safety, leaving a raw edge of fear and determination.

Lily and Max seemed to pick up on the tension, their usual morning cheer replaced with subdued whispers and uneasy glances in my direction. I tried to offer them reassuring smiles, but the effort felt hollow, the mask of confidence slipping.

On the way to school, every shadow seemed a lurking threat, every passing car a potential enemy. I walked briskly, my senses on high alert, guiding Lily and Max with a protective hand. I lingered longer than usual at the school gates, watching them disappear into the building, a gnawing worry in my stomach.

The hours at school dragged on, each minute stretching out with excruciating slowness. My focus was fractured, the words of teachers and peers sounding distant and muffled. My phone was a constant presence on the desk, a lifeline to the outside world, to the safety of Lily and Max.

After school, as we walked home, the sense of foreboding grew. I could feel the weight of unseen eyes on us, tracking our every move. Arriving home, I double-checked the locks and windows, a ritual that had become second nature.

The evening was tense, and dinner was eaten in uneasy silence. Lily and Max could sense the change, and their questions were growing more insistent. "Ethan, what's wrong? You're scaring us," Lily's voice quivered with fear and concern.

I knew I couldn't keep them in the dark any longer. "There's... someone who might be trying to scare us. But I've talked to the police, and we'll be fine. I'm here, and I'll always protect you," I said, my voice steady despite the turmoil inside.

As night fell, a sense of siege settled over our home. I kept the lights low, peering out the windows regularly, watching for any movement in the darkness. The hours ticked by, each one ratcheting up the tension.

Then, it happened. A shadow detached itself from the darkness across the street, moving stealthily towards our house. My heart leaped into my throat as I recognized the imminent threat.

I quickly ushered Lily and Max into the basement, instructing them to hide and keep quiet. "No matter what, stay here until I come for you," I said, my voice a mix of fear and authority.

I grabbed the baseball bat I kept for protection and moved towards the front of the house. The street was quiet, eerily so. Then came footsteps on the porch, a soft but unmistakable thud against the front door.

Adrenaline coursed through my veins as I positioned myself near the entrance, the bat gripped tightly in my hands. The door handle jiggled softly at the intrusion, followed by a more forceful shake.

I braced myself, ready to defend our home and protect Lily and Max at all costs. The door burst open, and I swung the bat with all my might, meeting the intruder with fierce resolve.

The Clash

In the dim light of the entryway, the bat connected with a solid thud, the sound reverberating through the quiet house. The intruder, a figure shrouded in darkness, staggered back, momentarily stunned. My heart pounded, a frantic drumbeat echoing the moment's chaos.

The intruder regained balance, lunging towards me with a grunt. I swung the bat again, fueled by adrenaline and the fierce instinct to protect my home and siblings. The bat hit its mark, sending the intruder reeling to the side.

A streetlight cast a sliver of light through the open door, illuminating the intruder's face. It was a face I didn't recognize, a stranger, but his eyes held a malicious intent that chilled my blood. He was not alone; another figure, equally determined and dangerous, appeared behind him.

I realized then that this was no random break-in. These were the shadows of my past, come to claim what they believed was owed. The reality of the situation hit me with a jolt – I was fighting for our lives.

The second intruder moved quickly, more agile than the first. He dodged my swing and landed a blow to my side. Pain shot through me, but it only fueled my resolve. I couldn't falter, not with Lily and Max hiding just a floor below.

Gritting my teeth against the pain, I swung again, my movements driven by a primal urgency. The bat connected with the second intruder, sending him crashing against the wall. The first intruder recovered, charging at me with renewed fury.

The fight was a blur of movement and desperation. I parried and struck, each blow, a statement of my refusal to let harm come to my family. The intruders were relentless, but so was I. The confined space of the entryway became a battleground, every object a potential weapon, every moment a fight for survival.

Suddenly, sirens wailed in the distance, growing louder with each passing second. The intruders hesitated, their resolve faltering as the reality of approaching law enforcement dawned on them.

Seizing the moment, I launched a final, powerful swing, knocking the bat against the nearest intruder's arm. He cried out, dropping a concealed knife to the floor with a clatter. The sound of it hitting the ground was a stark reminder of how close we had come to a different ending.

The intruders, realizing their time was up, scrambled away, disappearing into the night they had emerged from. I stood in the doorway, panting, the bat still in my hand, my body aching from the exertion and blows.

As the police arrived, flashing lights illuminating the street, I collapsed to my knees, the adrenaline leaving my body in a rush. Officers swarmed the house, their voices a cacophony of orders and questions. I could only think of Lily and Max, safe in the basement, unaware of how close danger had come.

Aftermath and Resolve

The aftermath of the night's confrontation was a whirlwind of flashing lights, concerned faces, and a barrage of questions from the police. As I sat in the back of the ambulance, a paramedic attending to the bruises and cuts, my mind was in a daze. The reality of what had transpired was still settling in, each moment replaying in my mind like a relentless echo.

An officer brought Lily and Max out from the basement, their faces pale and eyes wide with a mix of fear and relief. Seeing them safe and unharmed was a balm to the turmoil inside me. I embraced them, our hug a silent promise of protection and love.

Officer Daniels approached me, his expression a mixture of concern and professional detachment. "Ethan, you did good tonight. You protected your family. But this was too close. We need to ensure this doesn't happen again."

I nodded, the gravity of his words sinking in. The threats from my past life had finally caught up, and it was a stark reminder that the path I had chosen was fraught with danger, not just for me but also for Lily and Max.

The police took statements, their questions probing but gentle. I recounted the events, omitting the deeper involvement with Mr. Kline's world. I couldn't expose Lily and Max to that darkness, not when I had just fought so hard to protect them from it.

As the police wrapped up their investigation and the ambulance prepared to leave, I realized our home no longer felt like a sanctuary. The intrusion had shattered our sense of safety, leaving a tangible sense of vulnerability in its wake.

In the days that followed, the normal rhythm of life attempted to reassert itself, but everything was tinged with a sense of unease. Lily and Max were quiet, their usual playfulness dimmed by the shadow of the break-in. I reassured them as best I could, but the words felt hollow, even to my ears.

I knew that we couldn't stay in the house anymore. The risk was too significant, the memories too fresh. I started to arrange for us to move, to find a new place to start over, where the shadows of my past couldn't reach us.

The decision to leave was painful. This house was more than just walls and a roof; it was where we had shared laughter and tears, grieved our parents, and clung to each other in the aftermath. But the need to protect Lily and Max outweighed everything else.

We packed our belongings, each item a reminder of the life we were leaving behind. Lily and Max tried to be brave, but I could see the uncertainty in their eyes. I promised them that we would be together no matter where we went, that we were each other's home.

As we drove away from the house for the last time, I looked back at the fading silhouette of our home. A chapter of our lives had closed, marked by struggle, darkness, love, and resilience.

The road ahead was uncertain, filled with new challenges and changes. But I was determined to forge a better path for us, to leave the shadows of my past behind and build a future where fear and danger were no longer constant companions.

A New Beginning

The road to our new start was cloaked in a quiet sense of anticipation, each mile unfolding into landscapes alien and untouched by our history. Lily and Max, nestled in the backseat, absorbed the world rushing by with wide-eyed wonder, their trepidation about the unfamiliar slowly giving way to an adventurous spark.

We arrived in a small, picturesque town, its quaint streets and warmly lit shops promising a close-knit community shield from the echoes of our troubled past. Our new abode, a modest two-story house nestled on a serene street, greeted us with its cozy charm, a stark contrast to the grandiosity and shadows of where we'd been. Our neighbors' welcoming smiles and friendly waves infused our weary souls with a comforting warmth, an auspicious beginning to our fresh chapter.

The ensuing days were a blur of unpacking and nest-making, transforming the once empty spaces into a home vibrant with life and laughter. Lily and Max, their earlier hesitations dissolving, threw themselves into exploring every corner of our new sanctuary with gleeful abandon. Their seamless integration into the local school and the warm reception from the community filled me with an immense relief, watching them thrive and rediscover joy in their laughter and playful banter.

I found grounding in the rhythm of day-to-day life, my role at the local hardware store a far cry from the precariousness of my previous endeavors. Mr. Jacobs, the store's proprietor, extended a kindness and understanding that reached beyond the confines of our workplace, his wisdom a guiding light in moments of doubt.

Yet, as our lives began to weave into the fabric of this town, the shadows of our past loomed, a silent testament to the battles we'd endured. My nightly walks through the town became moments of reflection, the tranquility of our surroundings a bittersweet reminder of the peace we sought to preserve. Conversations with Officer Daniels, a steady anchor in the turbulent seas of our past, offered a semblance of security, a vigilant watch over the fragile serenity we'd built.

One evening, as I tucked Lily and Max into bed, their arms wrapped around me in a tight embrace, their whispers of gratitude echoed the depth of our journey. "Thank you, Ethan," they murmured, their voices a blend of strength and vulnerability that resonated deep within my soul. In their eyes,

I saw the reflection of our shared resilience, a bond forged in the crucible of adversity.

As I stood under the starlit sky, the quiet of the night enveloping me, I allowed myself to feel the weight of our journey and the promise of the road ahead. We had found a haven, a place to heal and rebuild away from the chaos that once threatened to consume us. Yet, I remained acutely aware that our journey was far from over, the path ahead fraught with unknowns.

But in the strength of our unity, the unwavering bond that tethered us, I found hope. Together, we would face whatever challenges lay ahead, our shared experiences a foundation upon which we would build our future. This new beginning was not just a chance to escape our past but an opportunity to redefine our destiny, guided by the lessons we'd learned and the love that sustained us.

Undercurrents of the Past

The sense of normalcy that had started to weave into the fabric of our daily lives in the new town was comforting. Yet, I couldn't shake off an undercurrent of tension. I watched Lily and Max with an overprotective eye, the scars of our past experiences etching a permanent mark in my psyche.

The autumn festival was a significant event in our new town, and the community buzzed with excitement as it approached. Lily and Max were caught up in the fervor, their enthusiasm contrasting to the apprehension that lingered in my heart.

The town square was transformed into a colorful tableau of stalls, games, and laughter on the festival day. The air was filled with the aroma of baked goods and the sound of live music. As we walked through the crowds, Lily and Max's faces lit up with joy, their laughter mingling with the festive atmosphere.

I tried to lose myself in the moment, to let go of the lingering fears. However, my eyes involuntarily scanned the crowd, searching for any signs of danger. The feeling of being watched by a ghost from the past still haunted me.

As the day wore on, I began to relax, the cheerful ambiance slowly chipping away at my defenses. We played games, sampled treats from the various stalls, and even enjoyed a hayride. Lily and Max's happiness was infectious, and for a brief moment, I allowed myself to forget the worries that had become my constant companions.

During the hayride, as we jostled along the scenic route on the outskirts of town, I noticed a figure standing at the edge of the woods. Distant and shadowy, it could have been anyone, yet a chill ran down my spine. My gaze lingered, but the figure disappeared, almost like it had been a figment of my imagination.

The rest of the evening passed with a vague sense of unease niggling at the back of my mind. I kept a close watch on Lily and Max, ensuring they were always within my sight. As the festival drew close, we joined the crowd in the town square for the fireworks display.

The night sky erupted in colors, each burst of light reflecting in Lily and Max's wide eyes. They were mesmerized, their faces aglow with wonder. I tried to focus on the moment's beauty, but the nagging worry refused to be quelled.

As I tucked them into bed that night, their excited chatter about the day's events filled the room. They were already looking forward to next year's festival. I smiled, promising them that we would be there.

Alone in the living room, the silence of the house enveloped me. The image of the shadowy figure by the woods lingered in my mind. Was it my imagination, or was the past reaching out to us in our new haven?

The day's events replayed in my mind as I lay in bed. The festival had been a beautiful experience, yet the brief sighting had stirred the embers of fear I had been trying to extinguish. I realized then that the shadows of our past were never far behind, always lurking at the edges of our newfound peace.

Unseen Threads

In the wake of the festival, a subtle yet unmistakable shift pervaded our new life. The fleeting glimpse of a figure at the woods' edge ignited a spark of vigilance in me, a reminder of the shadows we thought we'd outrun. While Lily and Max embraced their new beginnings with the innocence of youth, I found myself ensnared once more in a web of caution and wariness.

A morning encounter with an unfamiliar car loitering too close to comfort was the first in a series of unsettling occurrences. Its presence, possibly innocuous yet undeniably ominous, urged me to adopt old habits of surveillance and suspicion. This tension spilled over into my day, leaving me distracted and distant, a fact not unnoticed by Mr. Jacobs, whose concern I deflected with a strained smile.

The car's reappearance near our home later that day confirmed my fears—this was no coincidence. The sight of it through our living room curtains transformed the vehicle from a mere object into a symbol of looming danger. My call to Officer Daniels was a measured attempt to seek help without stirring undue alarm. His promise to investigate provided little solace, and the car's subsequent disappearance did nothing to ease my disquiet.

That night, the quiet of our home was a stark contrast to the storm of worry and speculation raging in my mind. Officer Daniels' follow-up call, intended to reassure, only served to deepen my unease. The mysterious car and the figure at the festival's edge were now intertwined in my thoughts, harbingers of a threat that seemed to be drawing ever closer, weaving its way silently into the fabric of our lives.

As darkness enveloped our home and I lay restless, the day's events coalesced into a chilling realization: our past, with its tendrils of fear and danger, might not be as far behind us as I'd hoped. The peace we'd fought so hard to find was fragile, and the specter of our old life lingered, a shadow waiting to emerge from the light.

Veiled Threats

The days unfolded under a shadow, the serene life we had begun to embrace in our small town now punctuated by a sense of looming danger. The mysterious car and the fleeting glimpse of a figure at the festival's edge had ignited a spark of unease that flickered persistently in my thoughts. Our newfound tranquility seemed increasingly fragile, a veneer over the reality of our past that refused to remain buried.

I found myself in a heightened state of alertness, accompanying Lily and Max to and from school with a vigilance that seemed to amuse them. They flourished in their new environment, their laughter and light-heartedness a stark contrast to the weight I carried within me—a weight forged from our past and the solemn duty to ensure their safety.

At the hardware store, my preoccupation did not escape Mr. Jacobs, whose concern for me was evident. "Ethan, you can talk to me if something's troubling you," he said, his voice embodying a fatherly warmth. Yet, I held back, wary of drawing anyone else into our circle of uncertainty. "Just some family stuff," I deflected, mustering a smile that failed to mask the turmoil beneath.

Walking home one afternoon, the familiar sensation of being watched prickled at my nerves. A quick glance revealed a figure vanishing as quickly as it appeared. Was this paranoia, or were we truly being monitored?

Back at home, I moved through the ritual of checking locks and windows, each click a feeble defense against the invisible threats encroaching on our peace. That evening, a chilling phone call shattered any remnants of denial. "You can run, but you can't hide. We're always watching," taunted a distorted voice before the line went dead. The reality was undeniable and terrifyingly close.

The decision to shield Lily and Max from the truth of the call was a heavy one, my silence a fortress I built around them. Yet, as I sat in the darkness, the quiet of our home belied the storm of worry and determination swirling within me. We had faced too much to allow shadows to reclaim us without a fight.

Determined, I resolved that action was necessary. The safety of my siblings was paramount, a beacon guiding me through the murk of fear and uncertainty. Confronting this hidden threat head-on was the only way forward, a path we would navigate together, fortified by the struggles we had already overcome and the unyielding bond that held us fast.

Stepping into the Shadows

The decision to confront the encroaching darkness head-on marked a pivotal moment in our lives. That restless night, as I strategized our next moves, the weight of the unknown pressed heavily upon me. The safety of Lily and Max, my beacon in the tumultuous sea of our past, propelled me forward, demanding a shift from defense to offense.

The following morning, after ensuring the kids were safely ensconced in the routine of school life, oblivious to the brewing storm, I sought the sanctuary of the local police station. The familiar yet imposing structure offered a semblance of hope, a potential ally against the veiled threats that loomed large.

Officer Daniels, a steadfast figure of authority and empathy, met my confession with a somber attentiveness. The revelation of another menacing call seemed to solidify his resolve, his assurance of increased surveillance a sliver of light in the gathering gloom. Yet, as I stepped back into the daylight, a gnawing unease remained. Our adversary, a specter from a life I had hoped to leave buried, remained just beyond reach, taunting us from the shadows.

Compelled by a desperate need to shield my family from further harm, I embarked on a journey into the heart of my former life. Mr. Jacobs, ever observant, could only offer his silent concern as I requested time away—a sabbatical marked not by rest but by a quest for answers deep within the underbelly of our past.

The drive to our old town was a pilgrimage through memories best forgotten, each mile a reminder of the choices and consequences that had led us to our current precipice. The familiarity of the landscape, now tainted by the shadow of our adversary, evoked a profound sense of dissonance. I was an interloper in my own history, returning not for nostalgia but for salvation.

The town itself seemed to hold its breath as I neared Mr. Kline's domain, a place that had once been a crucible of my transformation. The streets whispered secrets of a life I had narrowly escaped, and as I approached the nondescript façade of the building that had been the stage for much of my past dealings, a complex tapestry of emotions enveloped me.

Mr. Kline, a figure emblematic of my former existence, greeted me with a guarded mix of surprise and caution. His acknowledgment of the dangerous game I was playing—a game that now threatened the very fabric of my family's peace—was a testament to the gravity of our situation. His willingness to aid in my quest, however reluctant, was a beacon in the shadowy maze of our past entanglements.

As I left his presence, the burden of our perilous endeavor lay heavy on my shoulders. Stepping back into the darkness was a risk fraught with potential peril, but the stakes—Lily and Max's safety—were far too high. This path, shadowed and uncertain as it was, represented our only chance at reclaiming the light.

This juncture, a confluence of past and present, fear and hope, was more than a mere quest for answers. It was a crucible, testing the limits of my resolve and the depth of my love for Lily and Max. With each step taken back into the world I had forsaken, I was not just seeking the identity of our tormentor—I was fighting for the very soul of our family, determined to forge a future untainted by the specters of our past.

Unraveling the Knot

The drive back from the old town was a journey shrouded in contemplation. My meeting with Mr. Kline had reopened old wounds, but it was a necessary evil. The silence in the car was filled with the echoes of our conversation, each word a potential clue in unraveling the identity of the person threatening us.

Upon reaching our new home, Lily and Max playing in the yard, carefree and happy, solidified my resolve. I would go to any length to protect this picture of innocence and joy.

The following day was a Saturday. I spent it in a state of heightened alertness, balancing being a caring brother while watching for any signs of danger. Lily and Max seemed to sense my distraction, their playful banter occasionally pausing as they cast curious glances my way.

In the afternoon, my phone buzzed with a message from an unknown number. My heart raced as I opened it, but it was from Mr. Kline. "Got some info. Meet me tonight." The message was brief, but its implications were enormous.

As night fell, I left Lily and Max with Mrs. Henderson, our neighbor who had quickly become a friend and confidante. She was more than willing to watch them, believing I was attending to a mundane errand.

The meeting place Mr. Kline had chosen was an old warehouse on the outskirts of town. This place reeked of abandonment and forgotten stories. The building loomed in the darkness, its silhouette a menacing presence against the night sky.

Inside, Mr. Kline was waiting, his figure emerging from the shadows. "Ethan," he greeted, his voice echoing in the space. "I've done some digging. The threat isn't coming from within my circle. But I've heard rumors – someone from your past, not connected to us, has a vendetta against you."

The information sent a chill down my spine. Was it a vendetta from my past? The possibilities were numerous, each more unsettling than the last.

"Any idea who this person might be?" I asked, my mind racing through the list of potential enemies.

Mr. Kline shook his head. "No names, just whispers. Be careful, Ethan. This kind of grudge can be deadly."

I thanked him and left the warehouse, the night air feeling colder and heavier. The clarity I had hoped for was replaced by a more profound mystery that was personal and far more dangerous.

Back home, I checked in on Lily and Max, relief flooding me as I found them safe and sound, chatting animatedly with Mrs. Henderson. After ensuring they were settled for the night, I retreated to my room, my mind a whirlwind of thoughts.

The revelation that the threat was a personal vendetta complicated matter. It wasn't just a remnant of my past life in the criminal world; it was more intimate and targeted. I knew I had to tread carefully, unraveling this knot without exposing Lily and Max to the danger that lurked in the shadows.

The Revelation

The crescendo of tension that had been building reached its climax as I grappled with the shadows of my past, now threatening the tranquil life I had painstakingly built for Lily and Max. The enigmatic foe, whose identity eluded me, seemed both a specter from a life I yearned to forget and a stark reminder of the indelible marks our choices leave.

That night, as I delved into the annals of my past, sifting through names and faces that belonged to another era of my life, the reality of my actions and their consequences lay bare before me. The list of those I had wronged was a litany of my failings, a path marked by conflict and loss.

The breakthrough, when it came, was as shocking as it was illuminating—a distorted call that cut through the silence of the night, its message a harbinger of malice. "Ethan, you think you can just start over? You ruined my life. Now I'll ruin yours." The voice, though cloaked in electronic disguise, was unmistakably that of a former friend, a brother in arms turned adversary. His words were a knife to my heart, revealing the depth of the hurt and betrayal that festered like an unhealed wound between us.

This revelation brought a torrent of memories, of a friendship forged in adversity that had disintegrated under the weight of a single, calamitous decision. My actions, born of desperation, had inadvertently set him on a downward spiral from which he never recovered, transforming him into the nemesis who now sought to dismantle the semblance of peace I had built.

With this knowledge, I turned to Officer Daniels, seeking solace and resolution in the flickering neon glow of a diner's sign. I recounted my epiphany, each piece of the puzzle clicking into place with a resonance that felt like the tolling of a bell. Officer Daniels, ever the stalwart ally, listened with a gravity that mirrored my own. "We'll bring him in, Ethan. It's going to end now," he promised, his determination a lifeline in the storm that raged around us.

The day of reckoning was charged with a palpable tension. Officer Daniels and his team acted with commendable swiftness, apprehending the man who had once been a dear friend. The resolution was swift but far from simple; the confrontation that followed was a maelstrom of emotion—anger, grief, and a sorrowful recognition of what had been lost between us.

In the quiet aftermath, as I sat with Lily and Max, I found the strength to unveil the truths of our recent trials. With care, I unraveled the story of a friendship sundered by choices and the path to redemption that lay before us. They listened with a wisdom beyond their years, their faces etched with understanding and a quiet relief that the storm had passed.

That night, as I watched them drift into sleep, their faces unburdened by the shadows that had once loomed over us, a profound sense of closure enveloped me. We had weathered the tempest, confronted our past, and emerged not just unscathed but fortified by the ordeal.

As the dawn heralded a new day, I stood resolved to cherish and nurture the precious gift of peace we had reclaimed. With Lily and Max by my side, we would forge ahead, our bond a testament to the enduring power of love and forgiveness. The road ahead, once shadowed, now glimmered with the promise of hope, healing, and the unwavering conviction to build a future filled with joy and serenity.

The Aftermath

In the serene aftermath of our ordeal, each day brought a deeper healing, a gentle stitching of the fabric torn by fear and uncertainty. The threat that once cast a long shadow over our existence had dissipated, leaving behind a landscape of reflection and newfound strength.

Our return to the simple cadence of daily life in our quaint town offered a balm to the soul. The community, oblivious to the storms we weathered, continued to enfold us in a warm embrace of normalcy and acceptance. Back at the hardware store, Mr. Jacobs greeted me with a nod that spoke volumes, acknowledging the journey I had been on and welcoming me back to the sanctuary of routine and camaraderie. The familiar hum of life in the store, amidst tools and laughter, became a grounding force, anchoring me to the here and now.

Lily and Max, ever resilient, slipped back into their school lives with the grace and adaptability that never ceased to astonish me. They embraced our new reality with a vigor that belied their years, their spirits untainted by the shadows we had stepped out from. Watching them, I was reminded of the incredible capacity of youth to recover and find joy in the aftermath of turmoil.

As tranquility wove its way through the fabric of our days, optimism began to color my thoughts. The darkness that had once seemed endless was now behind us, clearing the path for a future bright with possibility. I found myself contemplating the horizon with a sense of hope, daring to dream of what lay beyond the immediate scope of our settled life.

One evening, gathered around the dinner table, Lily and Max's animated recounting of their day's adventures filled the room with a vibrant energy. Their laughter, pure and untethered, was a melody that spoke of security and happiness—a testament to the journey we had traversed. In their joy, I saw the reflection of our collective resilience, a beacon that had guided us through our darkest days.

Later, as I sat on the porch under a canopy of stars, the stillness of the night enveloped me. The peace that surrounded me was profound, a stark contrast to the tumult we had endured. In this quietude, I contemplated the future, a tapestry yet to be woven with threads of hope, challenges, and adventures. It was a moment of profound clarity, an understanding that our narrative was far from concluded.

As this chapter of our lives drew to a close, a profound sense of completion settled over me. We had navigated the depths of fear, faced down our demons, and emerged not just unscathed but fortified. Ahead lay a road unmarked, promising new journeys and trials, but the certainty that we would face them together filled me with an indomitable strength. Our past, with its lessons and battles, was now a foundation upon which we would build our future—a future we would embrace with open hearts and unwavering un